THE LITTLE FELLOW

By MARGUERITE HENRY

Illustrated by Rich Rudish

RAND McNALLY & COMPANY
CHICAGO · NEW YORK · SAN FRANCISCO

Copyright © 1975 by RAND McNALLY & COMPANY. All rights reserved.
Printed in the United States of America by RAND McNALLY & COMPANY.
LIBRARY OF CONGRESS CATALOG CARD NUMBER: 75-6828
First printing, July, 1975
Second printing, October, 1975
Third printing, August, 1976
Fourth printing, July, 1977

CHIP was a fuzzy little colt. He wasn't black. Nor was he brown. He was almost the same color as Chocolate, who was his mother.

Chocolate used to be a racehorse. But she never thought about winning races anymore.

All she thought about was her little colt, Chip.

Every morning the same thing happened to Chip. He opened his eyes to find himself curled up in a bed of straw.

The straw was warm . . . so warm and comfortable that Chip played make-believe. He closed his eyes, pretending sleep, feeling all safe and happy.

His mother knew he was just pretending. She nudged Chip with her nose, urging him up on his feet, talking continuously in deep, throaty tones.

Then she began to lick him all over.

First, she scrubbed his face and neck with her tongue. Then, his fuzzy coat. The more she licked, the fuzzier Chip grew.

Sometimes her tongue-strokes were so vigorous that Chip swayed like a sapling in the wind. It seemed as if she couldn't stop licking him.

But Chip didn't mind. He could have stayed there forever, enjoying her warm washcloth of a tongue.

Every now and then he'd nibble along Chocolate's silky neck. Chocolate often nipped him too. Her teeth were enormous, but she was oh, so gentle.

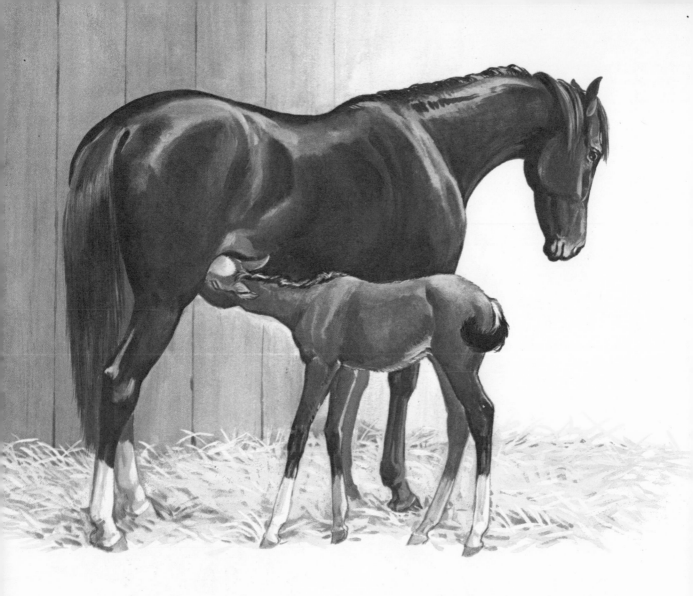

Chip's early morning bath made him feel frisky—*and* hungry. So he helped himself to his mother's milk until his sides were round as a barrel.

By this time in the morning Dooley, the stable hand, could be heard, whistling softly as he went about his work—filling water buckets, forking hay, measuring oats.

Soon Dooley's face appeared over the half door.

"Morning, Mrs. Choclit! Looks like you don't even miss yer racing days. And how's our little feller?" he asked as he poured oats into her feedbox. "Growing like a weed, you say? Well, then, let's give him a dab o' yer oats."

On the palm of his hand, Dooley offered a few grains. Chip tried to lip them, but they were hard and slippery. He liked warm milk better.

Dooley grinned. "Okay, Choclit, *you* show the little feller how to eat."

Chocolate needed no urging. With a noisy crunching she cleaned up all the oats in her box, then nosed in the straw for the grains Chip had dropped.

"See, Chip? That's the way a good eater does it!" Dooley gave Chocolate a pat of approval. Then he put on her halter and led her out into the warm sunshine.

Chip capered along at her side.

There were five or six other horses in the pasture, but Chip was the only baby.

This was his first spring. For the first time he heard the slurred whistle of a meadowlark. For the first time he smelled the sweetness of clover. He dipped his nose into a patch of it. He munched one or two of the bigger flowers, tasting the nectar.

"Hmmmmm . . . good!" he thought. "But I still like milk better."

He sniffed the faint perfume of apple blossoms in the distance. He ran. He jumped. He squealed. He bucked at nothing at all.

He was so happy that he rolled over on his back and kicked his legs wildly in the air.

How nice it felt to get the very center of his back scratched!

In the midst of his rolling, he suddenly stopped and listened to new strange sounds . . .

> the glug-glug of a bullfrog,
> the meowing of a catbird,
> the chattering of a squirrel.

Someday, when he had more time, he would find out where those noises came from.

A rabbit whiffed by, close to his whiskers. Chip was too comfortable, lying there in the sun, to chase him.

Instead he just snorted at him and whinnied fiercely.

Chip was making so much noise himself that he didn't hear Chocolate calling him. She had to neigh sharply to get his attention. "You! Young 'un! Come along!"

Chocolate and all the other horses were galloping toward the fence. "Cloppety! Cloppety!" went their big hoofs.

Chip hurried to catch up. "Clippety! Clippety!" went his little hoofs.

There at the fence stood The Family—The Man and his
Wife, and The Boy and The Girl.

The Family had brought little tidbits with them. There
were crisp carrots, juicy apples, and crunchy turnips for the
grown-up horses.

For Chip there was a tiny cube of sugar. Chip didn't
know which he liked better—the sugar, or the taste of The
Man's hand.

First, he curled his lips around the sugar, letting it melt on his tongue. When he'd swallowed the syrupy goodness, he licked The Man's hand, nodding his head at the salty taste. And The Man turned to his children.

"See that? The Little Fellow wants more!"

Then everyone began to praise Chip.

"What big eyes he has! And what lively ears!"

"He'll bring honor to Bluebell Farm."

"I love the white blaze on his face and his neat white socks," said The Girl.

"Oh, feel his whiskers and his fuzzy coat," cried The Boy.

The Family petted Chip. They stroked his neck and the white blaze on his nose. Their voices were soft and low, so Chip stood very still.

"Isn't he gentle!" said The Children.

"Ah, but he has fire and spirit," said The Man.

"He's a little beauty!" they all agreed.

Chip had no idea what they were saying, but he pricked his ears to catch every bit of the nice sound.

Every day The Family came and admired Chip. But even with all the attention he was getting, Chip was anxious to grow up.

He wanted to be as big as Chocolate and the other horses. He wanted to do what they did.

He wanted to bugle through his nose.

He wanted to sleep standing up.

He wanted to crop grass without losing his balance.

But more than anything else, Chip wanted to shoo flies with his tail—in the grand, swishy way the grown-ups did.

They made a regular ceremony of it!

At noontime—especially on hot, sultry days—the big horses gathered under the feathered shade of a honey locust tree. There they chose partners and teamed up, two by two.

What interested Chip was the way they stood. One partner always faced one way. The other faced the opposite way. Then when the flies began to buzz and bite, the horses' tails went *swish! swish!*

Each horse flicked flies from his own back, and from his partner's face.

It was like having two tails!

To Chip this seemed wonderful.

He longed to be a partner. He wanted to *swish swish* with his tail.

Of course, Chocolate let him stand close by her side, but she did all the swishing herself. The minute Chip flapped his tail, she shuddered her coat and walked away.

Chip wondered why.

One day when all the horses were napping in the shade of the honey locust tree, Chip noticed a big, round-barreled horse standing quite apart, looking very lonely.

It was Fanny Jenks.

She had no one to brush flies for her.

Chip watched her for some time. He saw a large horsefly light on her nose. Even when her head nodded as she dozed, the fly stuck on.

Chip suddenly had an idea. Little by little, he made his way over to Fanny Jenks. He was very quiet about it.

"This is going to be fun!" he thought. "Now *I* can be a partner."

Carefully, he sidled up to Fanny, placing his front feet alongside Fanny's back feet. He stood side by side with Fanny Jenks. Now he could shoo flies for Fanny, and Fanny could shoo flies for him.

But Chip forgot that he was just a little fellow.

He forgot that he was only half as tall as Fanny Jenks and only half as long.

He didn't know that his tail was short and frizzly, *and that it tickled!*

For a minute or two Fanny stood motionless. She kept right on napping.

Chip turned his head around. The fly was still on Fanny's nose, but it seemed more interested in rubbing its wings together than in biting. But suddenly—bzzz . . . zzz—a green-headed horsefly zoomed down on Fanny's back.

Swish! swish! went Fanny Jenks's tail. It felt silky as it brushed Chip's face.

Flappety! flappety! went Chip's wisp of a tail. It didn't begin to reach Fanny Jenks's back. It just grazed her belly, *and it tickled.*

With a snort, Fanny Jenks woke up. She jerked her head into the air. She laid her ears flat and snapped her jaws.

Chip froze in terror. His legs wouldn't move.

Fanny whirled, and with all the power of her hindquarters, she kicked out in fury.

A clump of earth flew against Chip's face.

"Oh, oh!" thought Chip. "I've got to get away from here!"

And he backed away as fast as he could until he ran into his mother.

For the rest of the afternoon, he stayed very close to Chocolate. He'd just let those flies bite Fanny Jenks. See if he cared!

A week went by without a glimpse of Fanny Jenks. Chip forgot all about her.

Then one morning she had a surprise for the other horses.

When Dooley led her out to pasture, a brand-new foal came wobbling along beside her.

Fanny neighed a cheery good morning to everyone. Then she pranced around the pasture as if she and her youngster were on parade.

Now it was Chip's turn to snort. He wrinkled his nose.

"Humph," he squeaked. "What a little thing! Why, he's so tiny he looks like a filly instead of a man-horse like me. He can't even keep his balance! His legs go scooting every which way."

Chip turned away with a tiny sneeze.

At that precise moment Chip heard voices and laughter. His ears pricked in expectancy. His heart beat faster.

Yes! Yes! It was The Family.

Oh, this was the best part of the day!

Chip could almost taste the sugar melting on his tongue. He could almost feel the soft hands stroking his neck. He could almost hear The Family say, "What a little beauty he is!"

The sound of those familiar voices was like the ringing of a dinner bell. From all over the pasture the horses came galloping.

"Cloppety! Cloppety!" went the big hoofs.

"Clippety! Clippety!" went Chip's hoofs.

But Fanny Jenks's colt made scarcely any thump at all.

Chip crowded to the front. He reached through the fence rails, his nose questing for sugar.

But something dreadful was happening.

The Family walked right past him, moving toward Fanny Jenks's baby.

"No two ways about it!" said The Man. "Here's an aristo-crat. He'll be a winner."

"His coat is almost red," said The Girl.

"Let's call him Strawberry," said The Boy. "Strawberry Jenks."

"What bold eyes he has! And what lively ears!" said The Man.

"He's a little beauty," they all agreed.

And the delicious sugar went to the new colt.

All Chip got was a sliver of dried apple.

Chip grew so angry he trembled. "I'll make The Family look at *me!*"

He stamped and pawed the earth. He raised his head and neighed sharply. To his surprise, he almost bugled through his nose.

But The Family laughed and laughed at him. "Why, I do believe The Little Fellow is jealous!" they said.

Even the horses laughed.

This was worse than not being noticed.

Chip had to do something to show how important he was. He edged his way along toward Strawberry Jenks. He nosed in between Fanny and Strawberry. Fanny was getting her share of the tidbits so she paid no attention to Chip.

Slyly, Chip nipped the baby colt, just a little nip.

Then he completely forgot himself and took a big bite.

He hadn't meant to bite so hard. Or had he?

Strawberry let out a whinny of terror.

"The big baby!" thought Chip. "For less than a turnip I'd chase him out of the pasture." He opened wide his jaws, baring his sharp, pincer teeth.

Strawberry jumped like a cat, and with a head start, ran for his life . . . along the fence line toward the lower end of the pasture. Chip was after him in a flash. Behind him he could hear the swift pounding of hoofs—Fanny's! She was chasing him! She would be on him in seconds.

On the other side of the fence, The Family was running after Strawberry. If he didn't stop he was going to crash into

the fence. Strawberry saw the danger. In panic he tried to jump over the fence, but he stumbled and somersaulted into the air, landing upside down under the rails.

Chip had to dig his hoofs into the turf to keep from piling on top of him.

Neither in nor out of the pasture, Strawberry was caught
fast. He looked funny there, like an overturned bug, squirming
and pawing the air. Chip laughed a high little horselaugh.

But it wasn't funny to Strawberry. He squealed loudly for
help.

Fanny Jenks hovered over him, trying her best to push him
up onto his feet. The Family tried too.

From all over the pasture, the other horses came at a gallop. The noise grew loud and louder. There were snortings, shrill whinnies, baby squeals, and Fanny's ringing neigh. There were thump-thumpings of many hoofs and the worried cries of The Family. All these noises echoed and multiplied into one great uproar.

Chip was amazed at all the hubbub one little bite had caused.

At last Dooley came running. He spoke soothingly as he untangled Strawberry's legs. Grasping the colt's forelegs in one hand and his hind legs in the other, he slid Strawberry out from underneath the fence to safety.

He really wasn't hurt much—just frightened.

As soon as Chocolate saw that Strawberry was all right, she bunted Chip with her nose. She bunted hard. Chip could tell that she was angry. She was pushing him to the far end of the pasture.

When she had him alone, she scolded him in whuffs and grunts that were plainer than any words.

"Chip! Where in tunket is your horse sense? Strawberry Jenks is just a baby. You're almost grown up. This is a wide pasture, Chip. There's room for you, and Strawberry too."

Chip nodded in agreement with everything Chocolate said.

Yes, he knew Strawberry was only a baby.

Yes, he knew he might have caused Strawberry to break a leg.

Yes, he supposed The Family *could* like two colts equally well—as soon as the newness wore off Strawberry.

Chocolate had never scolded Chip before. He felt more ashamed by the moment. If only he didn't have to face the other horses!

With head low and tail drooping, he walked slowly to his stall. But the door was closed for the day.

He wished for night when he could hide in the darkness where no one would ever find him.

He moped and brooded, crying in little colt whinners. No one seemed to care for him anymore.

The time of misery for Chip stretched from hours to days. His mother didn't even comfort him with her tongue anymore. She sometimes seemed more interested in Fanny's colt than in him.

He would notice her ears moving back and forth to catch everything The Family said about Strawberry.

At night, Chip began to roll in his stall.

"Land sakes!" said Dooley. "Is he going to be a nervous tumblebug all his life?"

"Tumblebug, my eye!" thought Chip.

The days came and went, growing warmer and sultrier.

Young Strawberry Jenks sometimes left his mother's side and went off on little exploring trips. He even tried to be friends with Chip.

But try as Chip would, he could not feel friendly toward Strawberry.

Instead, he kicked up his heels and ran the other way. Then he'd turn around and snort at Strawberry.

One hot, windless morning when the flies began to buzz and
bite earlier than usual, the horses stopped grazing in the sun.
Lazily they ambled over to the shade of the honey locust tree.

"Clop! Clop!" went their big hoofs.

"Clippety! Clippety!" went Chip's little hoofs.

But the hoofs of Strawberry Jenks made scarcely any sound
at all.

As if by a signal, the grown horses lined up two by two in the cool shade.

Chip noticed that his mother had chosen Fanny Jenks as a partner.

Fanny was brushing flies for Chocolate, and Chocolate was brushing flies for Fanny.

Swish! swish! went their tails.

Chip was left to himself. He closed his eyes to shut out his aloneness.

Suddenly a warm body rubbed against his own. How nice and fuzzy it felt! *"Somebody's chosen me!"*

Without looking, he knew it was Strawberry Jenks.

"Why, my stars!" thought Chip. "Strawberry is almost as tall as I am. He's almost as long as I am. He's practically the right size."

Just then a swarm of horseflies came buzzing over and around and on them. Some were fierce biters.